MOKIE & BIK

Go to Sea

Wendy Orr

illustrations by Jonathan Bean

Henry Holt and Company · New York

*To James and Susan, who grew up far from the sea
but had lots of adventures in boats —W. O.*

Henry Holt and Company, LLC, *Publishers since 1866*
175 Fifth Avenue, New York, New York 10010
www.HenryHoltKids.com

Henry Holt® is a registered trademark of Henry Holt and Company, LLC.
Text copyright © 2010 by Wendy Orr
Illustrations copyright © 2010 by Jonathan Bean
Library of Congress Cataloging-in-Publication Data
Orr, Wendy.
Mokie and Bik go to sea / Wendy Orr ; illustrations by Jonathan Bean.—1st ed.
p.   cm.
Summary: With their father home from the sea, the rambunctious twins Mokie and
Bik make the Bullfrog shipshape for a voyage out to sea, where they make friends
with a scaredy-seal, save a runaway boat, and keep track of Waggles.
ISBN 978-0-8050-8174-9
[1. Twins—Fiction. 2. Brothers and sisters—Fiction. 3. Boats and boating—Fiction.
4. Humorous stories.] I. Bean, Jonathan, ill. II. Title.
PZ7.O746Mos 2008   [Fic]—dc22   2007027590

First Edition—2010
Printed in February 2010 in the United States of America by
Worzalla Publishing Company Inc., Stevens Point, Wisconsin
1 3 5 7 9 10 8 6 4 2

Contents

Waggles Overboard!

Mokie and Bik lived on a boat called *Bullfrog*. They lived in it, on it, all around it—monkeying up ladders and

down

ropes,

over the wheelhouse and across the cabin floor.

"Twins!" their father shouted,
because he was Charting and their
mother was Arting. "Get out from
underfoot!"

So Bik and Mokie frogleaped out
the door, boing-bounding over sleepdog Laddie, boing-bouncing around
Slow the tortle.

Waggles boinged out the door
after them—*splash!*—into nanny Ruby's
bucket as she was sploshing the deck.
  "Waggles!" shouted Ruby. "Get
out from underfoot!"

The bucket rolled down the deck.
Waggles scrabble waggle scrabbled.
The water swished over the slippy
wet deck, swoshed over Mokie's and
Bik's soggy socks—and then Waggles
skiddled out of the bucket, across the
deck and—*splash!*—into the sea.

"Waggles!" shouted Mokie.

"Overboard!" shouted Bik.

Bik and Mokie skiddled across the deck, over the rail, and—*splash!*—into the sea.

"Twins overboard!" shouted Ruby, grabbing her boathook.

"Twins overboard?" asked Dad, jumping up from his Charts.

"Twins overboard?" echoed Mom, peering over her Art.

But Mokie and Bik bobbed back up, and so did Waggles.

Waggles had black curly hair and big black paddly paws to help him swim. When he grew up he was going to be a swimming, rescuing

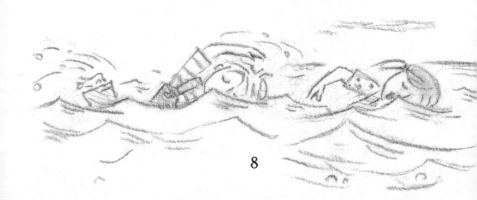

Newfoundland dog. But right now
he was a soggy shaggy round black
waggles, and he knew how to swim
but he didn't know which way to go.

So Waggles mad scrabble paddled
straight out to sea—and Mokie and
Bik splash paddled after him.

Ruby reached with her boathook to
fish the twins out by their overall
straps—but Mokie and Bik paddled
right past.

Waggles scrabble paddled fast, and
Bik and Mokie splash paddled faster.
They grabbed Waggles before he got
to the middle of the harbor.

Mokie held Waggles under one arm and paddled with the other—but it was hard to swim with a soggy shaggy round black waggles under one arm.

"*Tadpole*!" panted Bik.

"Quick!" puffed Mokie.

Bik paddled as fast as a fisk, flick kick swick, back to the rowboat tied behind *Bullfrog*. He monkeyed in, untied the rope, and row-row-row-boated back to Mokie and Waggles.

Waggles was still scrabbling. Mokie was still paddling and swallowing big mouthfuls of harbor.

Bik pulled Waggles's shaggy shoulders and Mokie pushed his round black bottom till Waggles tumbled into *Tadpole*.

Then Mokie scrabbled, Bik pulled, Waggles barked, *Tadpole* tip tip tipped . . . and Mokie slid in, too.

Bik rowboated back to *Bullfrog* and tied *Tadpole* to her stern.

Ruby put down her boathook.

Their mother picked up her brush.

Their father pulled Waggles onto *Bullfrog*. Mokie and Bik monkeyed up after him, and they all lay together like slippery fisk in the sunshine on the slippy wet deck.

Shipshaping Bullfrog

When Mokie and Bik's father was
sailing his ship-at-sea, far, far away
on the illy-ally-o, *Bullfrog* stayed tied
to the wharf. All she could do was
rollick and roll when Erik the Viking's
seagull boat chugged past, or the
police boat or the ferry, and roll and
rollick when their mother came home
on her botormike and jumped back on
board.

But now Mokie and Bik's father
was home to be Captain.

"So *Bullfrog*," said Mokie.

"Can go to sea," said Bik.

Bik and Mokie could jump into
Tadpole and row-row-rowboat to the
end of the wharf and back again, or
row-row-rowboat to the beach and
back again. But the big ships brooped
if *Tadpole* got to the middle of the
harbor, and Mokie and Bik had to
rowboat as fast as they could back to
the wharf.

"When I'm big,"
said Bik, "I'll sail
right around the
harbor."

"When I'm
bigger," said
Mokie, "I'll
sail right
around the
world!"

14

Their father had sailed right around the world. His ship-at-sea had clouds of sails on five tall masts and a brrr-ooping broop for fog.

"It's a parrot ship," said Mokie.

"It's where he keeps his pirate and the treasure on his chest," said Bik.

"Barnacle bells!" said Dad. "What are you twins yabbering about?"

Dad didn't want anyone to know he was a parrot. That's why he brought Waggles when he came home to *Bullfrog*, instead of a pirate named Jezebel.

Waggles was better than pirates or treasure. "But if I had a pirate I could teach it to yabber," said Bik.

"If I had a treasure I could buy chocolate and botormikes," said Mokie.

"So we need," said Bik.

"To go to sea," said Mokie.

"We'll go to sea," said Dad, "when *Bullfrog*'s shipshape."

"Let's," said Mokie.

"Yes!" said Bik.

So Bik and Mokie shipshaped up and down the deck, slip slide slippering from bow to stern, monkey thump clunking down to the engine room.

"Don't touch the engine!" shouted Dad.

So Mokie shipshaped up to the wheelhouse to spin the wheel, steering veering peering out the windows, wiggling *Bullfrog*'s throttle and big brass gearstick.

"Don't touch the gearstick!" shouted Dad.

Bik shipshaped down to the wharf and grabbed the rope that was tied to the very front of *Bullfrog*. "Casting off the forward line!" he shouted.

"Don't touch the lines!" shouted Dad.

So Mokie and
Bik found a long
hairy rope that
nobody wanted
and shipshaped
up to the very
front point of the bow.
They tied the rope around the
anchor, crank hank yanking it tight.

They monkeyed the other end up
to the wheelhouse roof, looping it
around the railing, with a long rope
tail behind.

Bik swung down on the rope's long
tail, swing ping zinging off the wheelhouse roof, ping zing swinging over
the deck, over the rail and over the
sea, pinging back—*crash!*—against
Bullfrog's side.

Mokie s-t-r-e-t-c-h-e-d over the wheelhouse roof, grabbed the long hairy rope with Bik on the end, and jumped—*thump!*—to the deck.

The rope swung Bik up and over the rail—*thump!*—to the deck on top of Mokie. Waggles jumped—*thump!*—lick wiggle on top of Bik, and they all crashed together in a jiggly heap.

Ruby was sploshing dishes in the galley and singing, "I'se the bye that catches the fish and takes them home to Lizer."

"Twins!" she shouted. "What are you doing?"

"Shipshaping," shouted Mokie and Bik, "so *Bullfrog* can go to sea."

A Lot to Learn

Waggles had:
    thick black curly hair,
    a quick licky tongue,
    big black paddly paws,
    and A Lot to Learn!
That's what Mokie and Bik's mother said, and their father, and Ruby. It's what Laddie growled, too.

Slow just pulled his head under his shell.

Waggles stole tubes of paint, oozing squoozing red and yellow, sticky icky fur and paws, across the wheelhouse floor and wheelhouse walls.

"No, Waggles, NO!" shouted Mom.

Waggles skiddled out the wheelhouse door, found a rope with a bumper on the end, and tug grrr thumped it onto the deck—the bumper  that stopped *Bullfrog* from thump bump WHUMPING onto the wharf.

"No, Waggles, NO!" shouted Dad.

Waggles skiddled across the deck where Ruby was polishing *Bullfrog*'s

big brass bell and whatumacallits, and
he started to pee on the galley hatch.

"No, Waggles, NO!"
shouted Ruby, grabbing
Waggles and holding him
out over the side.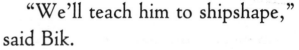

So Bik and Mokie
took Waggles and they
all skedaddled to the
beach.

"We'll teach him to shipshape,"
said Bik.

They monkeyed up on top of a
long fat log. Bik balanced on one
end, Mokie on the other, and
Waggles scrabbled in between.

"Waggles!" said Mokie.

"COME!" said Bik.

Waggles scrabbled in the middle
and didn't know which way to go.

Erik the Viking's seagull boat
chug-chug-chugged back to the
wharf. Bik and Mokie waved, and
Erik the Viking waved back.

Erik the Viking's big ginger hisser
jumped off the seagull boat onto the
wharf.

Waggles frogleaped off the log,
across the beach, and down the
wharf skid skad skedaddle after the
big ginger hisser.

"Waggles!" shouted Bik.

"COME!" shouted Mokie, but
Waggles was chasing too fast to hear.

Waggles chased the hisser and
Mokie and Bik chased Waggles up

the wharf and down again until the
hisser turned and went *sss-sss-hiss* at
Waggles.

Waggles skedaddled back quick to
Bik and Mokie.

"Good Waggles!" said Bik.

"He came!" said Mokie.

They monkeyed back onto *Bullfrog*.
Ruby was singing "I'se the bye that
builds the boat" and chopping meat in
the galley.

Waggles scrabbled down the ladder
to see her—but Sleepdog Laddie
barked, "Get back on deck!" and
Slow the Tortle pulled his head under
his shell. So Waggles scrabbled back
up to Mokie and Bik.

"It's hard for a waggles," said
Mokie.

"To be good," said Bik.

At bunktime, Mokie and Bik made a bed for Waggles between their bunks at the very V of the bow, so they could whisper to him at night.

But Waggles whined a lonely whine, because he was on the floor and Bik and Mokie were up too high to reach.

Bik hung upside down from his knees over the edge of his bunk to pat Waggles's curly black head. Waggles jumped into his arms, and Bik tumbled—*thump clunk* overbunk— to the floor.

"What's that noise?" shouted Dad.

"Nothing," said Mokie and Bik.

Bik pulled Waggles's shaggy shoulders and Mokie pushed Waggles's round black bottom and Waggles tumbled into Bik's bunk. He curled up beside Bik and went to sleep.

The next night Waggles scrabbled up the steps to Mokie's bunk and curled up with her, and the night after that, with Bik.

Waggles never forgot whose turn it was.

Saving Bullfrog

One bright breezy morning Mokie and Bik's mother jumped on her botormike, roaring brrr-oaring down the road with her easel and Laddie in the sideboat.

Ruby walked down the wharf and onto a streetcar to the town where

children lived in their houses-on-the-ground and so did Ruby's mother.

"And we're taking *Bullfrog* to the fuel barge," said Dad, "to fill up her fuel."

The fuel barge was far, far away from the wharf, out where the harbor met the sea.

"Nearly," said Bik.

"On the illy-ally-o," said Mokie.

"Time to shipshape!" said Dad. "All hands on deck!"

Bik and Mokie clap slap clapped hands up and down the deck with Waggles shipshaping behind.

Dad untied *Tadpole* from *Bullfrog*'s stern and tied her to the wharf.

"Bik!" shouted Dad. "Throttle!"

Bik ran to the wheelhouse, and when Dad started the engine chug thump chugging, Bik wiggled the throttle till the chugging was quiet as a hisser's purr.

"But DON'T touch the gearstick!" said Dad. "I don't want *Bullfrog* to take off without me!"

Bik looked at the big brass gearstick, but he didn't touch it.

"Mokie!" shouted Dad. "Casting off!"

Mokie frogleaped from the deck to the wharf.

"Cast off the spring line!" Dad shouted.

Mokie undid the rope that tied the wharf to *Bullfrog*'s middle.

"Cast off the forward line!" Dad shouted.

Mokie untied the very front rope and shipshaped back up the ladder to *Bullfrog*, because she didn't want to be left all alonely on the wharf.

"I'm casting off the aft line!" Dad shouted. He untied the rope at the end of *Bullfrog* and frogleaped back onto the deck.

Then Waggles saw Erik the Viking's big ginger hisser walking down the wharf.

Waggles jumped at the hisser, off *Bullfrog*, and onto the wharf.

Dad shouted, "Waggles, come!" and jumped off *Bullfrog* and onto the wharf—*whumpf!*—on his bottom.

"Waggles, COME!"
shouted Mokie. "*Bullfrog*'s
ready to chug!"

Waggles already knew how to:
    sit and beg,
    climb ladders,
    and stay out of Laddie's way
        when Laddie was snozzing.

But Waggles could never remember
how to stop when he was chasing that
big ginger hisser.

"Waggles, COME!" Bik shouted
from the wheelhouse, LOUD, LOUD,
LOUD!

The twins were calling Waggles so hard that even when they felt *Bullfrog* drifting away, they didn't see Dad sitting on the wharf.

Mokie went back to the wheelhouse.

"I'm Captain!" said Bik, spinning the wheel.

"Don't touch the gearstick!" said Mokie, and Bik tried to look as if he hadn't wanted to anyway.

"Where's Dad?" asked Bik.

"Shipshaping the bumpers," said Mokie, so Bik fiddled the throttle and turned the wheel while he was still Captain.

Then he looked behind him through the wheelhouse window and saw *Bullfrog*'s bumpers bump thump whumping on her side, and saw the wharf too far away to whump against.

"The bumpers aren't shipshaped!" said Bik. "WHERE'S Dad?"

Mokie ran from the bow to the stern and back again, from the wheelhouse to the galley to the engine room—but she couldn't find Dad, and now they were drifting, wibble wobble wallowing way out in the harbor.

Bullfrog was easy to steer when the engine was chugging, but when the engine purred gently as a hisser and the gearstick didn't tell her whether to go forward or back, *Bullfrog* wibble wallowed lazy as a bathtub. The waves wobbled her where they wanted to go—and no matter how hard he stared at the gearstick, Bik didn't know whether to push it or pull.

"Drop the anchor!" shouted Bik, but it was too heavy to lift.

"Go back to the wharf!" shouted

Mokie, but the wind and waves were too strong.

"We'll have to—" said Bik.

"Yes," said Mokie, and Bik pointed *Bullfrog* toward the fuel barge.

Mokie skiddled to the bow, waving on her sliptoes at the very front point. "Help!" she shouted.

The barge man smiled and waved back.

Now the wind whistled stronger, and *Bullfrog* wibble wallowed faster. The sea on the other side of the barge came closer and the waves rollicked higher.

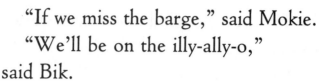

"If we miss the barge," said Mokie.

"We'll be on the illy-ally-o,"
said Bik.

"And we might never come back,"
said Mokie.

They were nearly at the fuel barge.
"Slow down!" shouted Mokie.

Bik couldn't slow down but he was
still Captain; he felt very important and
very small. He spun the wheel hard.

Bullfrog turned and wibble wallowed gently against the barge.

Mokie threw *Bullfrog*'s forward rope to the barge man. He pulled it tight and said, "Twins! What are you doing on the deck all alone? Where's your dad?"

"We lost him," said Mokie and threw the rope at the very back of *Bullfrog*.

"He must have overboarded,"
said Bik.

"We didn't mean to!" said Mokie.

The barge man chuckled from his
boots to his beard. "You're heroes!"
he said. "You saved *Bullfrog*."

Mokie and Bik didn't want to be
heroes with an overboard dad. Bik
threw the middle rope, and they tried
not to cry.

"Look!" said the barge man.

There was *Tadpole* skiddling across the harbor, with Dad row-row-row-boating and Waggles waggling in the stern.

A Bottle from a Parrot

"Today," said Bik.

"We can go to sea," said Mokie.

"With Dad," said Bik. "And Mom and Ruby."

"And Laddie and Waggles and Slow," said Mokie, because they didn't want to be all alonely on the illy-ally-o.

But first, Ruby had to splosh *Bullfrog* from one end to the other.

Mokie and Bik helped, splosh swosh galoshing from the wheelhouse wall to the pointy bow, swosh glosh spaloshing down the decks to the stern—and Waggles helped, too.

"Twins!" shouted Ruby. "Get out from underfoot!"

So they monkeyed down to the galley where their mother was mixing butter and flour and eggs for a cake.

Bik and Mokie helped, swishing flour and splashing eggs—and Waggles helped, too.

"Twins!" shouted their mother. "Get out from underfoot!"

Mokie and Bik skiddled into the engine room where Dad was ship-shaping *Bullfrog*'s engine with sticky oil and slimy grease.

"Twins!" shouted Dad, before they could touch. "Get out from underfoot!"

"Let's," said Bik.

"Yes!" said Mokie, and they monkeyed down into *Tadpole* with Waggles, because Laddie and Slow wouldn't come. Bik sat on the seat and rowboated, Mokie kneeled in the bow with the fisk net, and Waggles waggled in the stern.

Bik rowboated around the wharf's fat barnacled legs.

Mokie swished her net through a cloud of tiny fisk, but the fisk all swicked away.

Waggles barked at a starfish, but he didn't catch it.

Mokie swished her net swish wish
swish through a slime of weaseed, but
the weaseed washed right through
and her net was slimy green.

"Look!" said Bik.

"Let's!" said Mokie.

A small blue bottle was bobbling
on the harbor.

Bik row-row-rowboated and Mokie
knelt in the bow with her net swish
wishing. Waggles waggled and the
bottle bobbled.

"Ready!" said Bik.

"Got it!" said Mokie, swishing a
slippy drippy bottle into her net.

"It might have a message," said
Mokie.

"From a parrot," said Bik. "It
might be a map for treasure on his
chest."

Mokie opened the bottle, but there
was nothing inside except sniff whiff
stinky salty slime.

"I think his pirate ate it," said Bik.

"I think he found his treasure,"
said Mokie.

"When I'm big," said Bik, "I'm going to find bottles with messages."

"When I'm bigger," said Mokie, "I'm going to find parrots with maps for treasure."

"Twins!" shouted Ruby. "*Bullfrog*'s ready to go to sea!"

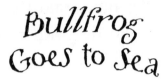

Bullfrog Goes to Sea

Bullfrog was ready to chug.

"Mokie!" shouted Dad. "Throttle!"

Mokie skiddled to the steering drawers. She held Waggles tight with one hand and wiggled the throttle with the other.

"Bik!" shouted Dad. "Cast off the forward line!"

Bik frogleaped from the deck to the wharf and untied *Bullfrog*'s very front rope.

"Cast off the spring line!" Dad shouted.

Bik untied the middle rope and monkeyed back quick onto *Bullfrog*'s deck.

"I'm casting off the aft line!" Dad shouted and untied the rope at *Bullfrog*'s stern.

Dad frogleaped back up on deck. He took the wheel and pushed the big brass gearstick. *Bullfrog*'s engine thump-thump-thumped right up through their feet.

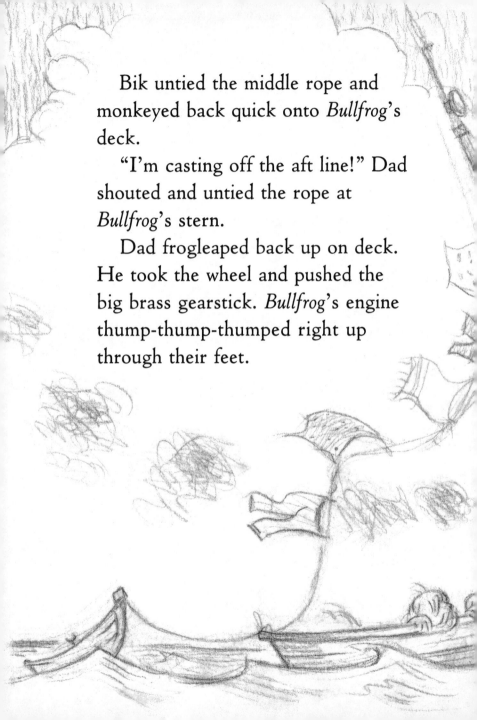

"It's *Bullfrog*'s heart," said Mokie.
Bullfrog chug-chug-chugged away
from the wharf into the harbor with
Tadpole rollicky frolicking behind at
the end of her rope.

Sleepdog Laddie was snozzing on the deck in the sun. Bik and Mokie took Waggles and Slow up to the very front point of the bow so *Bullfrog* could shiver their timbers, thump clunk whumping across the waves.

They passed the islands that were bigger than rocks but smaller than *Bullfrog*.

"Mine's starboard," said Mokie.

"Mine's port," said Bik.

They passed the fuel barge, and the barge man waved and tooted his toot. "Ahoy, *Bullfrog*!" he shouted.

"Ahoy, Barge Man!" Bik shouted back.

Bik's voice was LOUD, LOUD, LOUD. "Louder than a foghorn," said Dad.

They passed the lightflash house
with the red light flashing on top.
"Ahoy, Lightflash Man!" Bik
shouted, and the lightflash man
waved back.

They chug-chug-chugged right out of the harbor, where the deep-sea waves rollicked from far, far away on the illy-ally-o. *Bullfrog* slid up and thumped down, splashing waves over the bow.

Waggles barked at the waves.

Slow pulled his head in under his shell.

Bik and Mokie soggy sock skated down the slippery wet deck, past the wheelhouse and down to the stern, and Waggles skated, too.

"Look!" said Mokie.

"A neagle!" said Bik.

The neagle swooped on wide black wings. It circled low above *Bullfrog*. It dived with yellow claws out over Slow the Tortle.

Sleepdog Laddie sprang to his feet. He grrr roar growled deep and loud. He raced to the bow where Slow was snozzing.

The neagle soared into the sky and disappeared.

Laddie picked up Slow in his mouth and carried him back to the wheelhouse.

Bik and Mokie monkeyed down to the galley and back to the wheelhouse with a piece of meat for Laddie and another one for Slow.

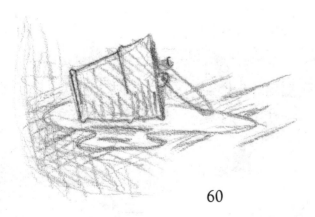

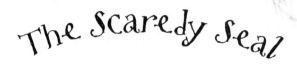

The Scaredy Seal

Bik and Mokie sat out on the deck
in the sun, as good as gold for about
twenty hours till the land was gone.

"Let's," said Bik.

"Yes!" said Mokie.

They slippered down the deck,
quiet as secrets in their soggy socks,
past the wheelhouse where Dad was

steering, Mom was Arting, and Laddie, Waggles, and Slow were snozzing, past the galley window where Ruby was sploshing the dishes.

Mokie and Bik stood at the very back of *Bullfrog* and watched *Tadpole* rollicky frolicking at the end of her rope.

Bik tug-tug-tugged the rope till *Tadpole* was nearly touching *Bullfrog*. "Now!" said Bik.

He held the rope tight and Mokie
swung down it into *Tadpole*.

Bik followed quick, but the rope
got longer and Bik swung wilder,
swish swing slipping into the waves.

Mokie grabbed the rope and tug-
tug-tugged till Bik tumbled into
Tadpole.

"Whew!" said Bik.

"NO!" shouted Mokie, because
Waggles was waggling under the rail
to follow.

Bik grabbed the rope and tugged
again.

Waggles overboarded—*thump!*—into
Mokie's arms, and they all tumbled
wiggle jiggle giggle into the bottom
of *Tadpole*.

Tadpole rollicky frolicked across

the waves, splashing spraying, kerplashing playing.

Then their timbers shivered with another *thump!* A silvery seal slipped over the side into *Tadpole*.

Bik and Mokie looked at the seal and it looked at them.

Waggles barked at the seal and it barked at him.

The seal's eyes were big and brown and round, and it was huff puff panting hard and loud.

"It's a scaredy seal!" said Mokie.

"Look!" said Bik.

A normous scormous black and white head poked out of the waves, a normous black eye looked all around.

Then the normous scormous eee-normous black, white, and shiny whale jumped out of the water and splashed a normous scormous EEE-NORMOUS splash.

"Barnacle bells!" shouted Bik, and so did Mokie.

The water sprayed. *Tadpole* rollicky frolicked till she tip slip tipped, Waggles and the seal squig wig jiggled, and Mokie and Bik clung tight as barnacles to *Tadpole*'s side.

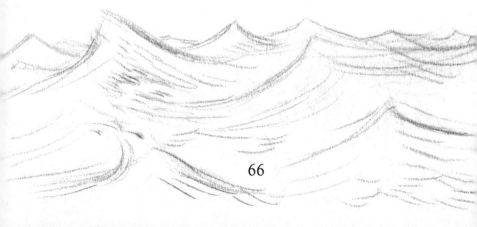

Bullfrog rollicked. Ruby raced to the bow to find Mokie and Bik, but they were gone.

"Twins overboard!" shouted Ruby, snatching up her boathook.

"With the whale?" asked Mom, rushing to the side as the normous scormous eee-normous whale sank under the sea.

"Where?" shouted Dad, slowing *Bullfrog*'s engine.

"Rowboating!" shouted Mokie.

"With a scaredy seal!" shouted Bik.

"Barnacle bells!" said Dad.

Bik and Mokie were soggy, their knees were wobbly and their teeth were chattery and they didn't want to go rowboating anymore. So Dad tug-tug-tugged *Tadpole* right up to

Bullfrog, Waggles licked the scaredy
seal good-bye, and Mom and Dad and
Ruby pulled them back up on deck.

And the seal flippered out of
Tadpole and into the sea.

When *Bullfrog* had been chugging for a long, long day, Mokie looked through the big oculars and saw a beach on an island not very far away.

"Please, can we?" said Mokie.

"Go to the beach?" said Bik.

"We can dig for clams!" said Mom.

"And I'll cook them for dinner," said Ruby.

"Mokie saw the beach," said Dad. "So she can steer."

Mokie monkeyed up the steering drawers and captained *Bullfrog* toward the beach.

Dad switched off the engine and rattled the anchor down to the bottom of the sea so *Bullfrog* couldn't float away, all alonely on the illy-ally-o.

Bik monkeyed
into *Tadpole* and
picked up the oars.
Ruby climbed into
Tadpole's stern
and Mom climbed
into the bow. Bik rowboated them
all to the beach, and when Mom and
Ruby splashed out, he rowboated
back for Dad and Mokie, and for
Laddie, Waggles, and Slow, and for
the buckets and spades.

Bik rowboated them all right to the
beach and dragged *Tadpole* up onto
the sand.

The sand was sticky wet with small bubbling holes, squirt spurting water into the air and up Bik's overall's leg.

Bik jumped.

"A clam found you!" said Mom, and started to dig.

The clams squirt swirt spurted, and Bik and Mokie dug-dug-dug. Waggles dug-dug-dug, too, spraying sand and splashing waves till his holes filled up with water.

Laddie dug a hole to snoz in, and Slow walked in the sand, slow slow slow.

When the buckets were full, Dad made a bonfire and cooked the clams and everyone munch lunch crunched around the fire. The sky turned pink-gold-black, the waves hush slush shushed against the sand, and the moon and the stars danced in the water.

Late, late at night they rowboated back to *Bullfrog* and monkeyed up on deck.

"Bunktime!" said Mom.

Mokie and Bik lay in their bunks in the bow, as good as gold for about twenty hours, but they couldn't sleep.

"Let's," said Bik.

"Yes!" said Mokie.

They took their blankets from their bunks and curled up on the deck with Waggles snuggling in between and the engine thumping like *Bullfrog*'s heart.

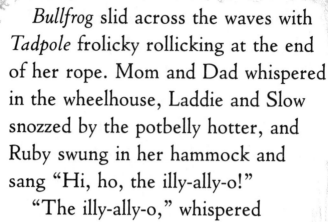

Bullfrog slid across the waves with *Tadpole* frolicky rollicking at the end of her rope. Mom and Dad whispered in the wheelhouse, Laddie and Slow snozzed by the potbelly hotter, and Ruby swung in her hammock and sang "Hi, ho, the illy-ally-o!"

"The illy-ally-o," whispered Mokie.

"Tomorrow," said Bik.

"Let's," said Mokie.

"Yes," said Bik, and they went to sleep.